P9-AQD-236

Pokémon
DP BATTLE DIMENSION

The Pokémon Sneak

BASED ON THE EPISODE "IF THE SCARF FITS, WEAR IT!"

SCHOLASTIC INC.

New York   Toronto   London   Auckland
Sydney   Mexico City   New Delhi   Hong Kong

ISBN: 978-0-545-17725-2

12 11 10 9 8 7 6 5 4 3 2 1   10 11 12 13 14 15/0

Designed by Henry Ng
Printed in the U.S.A.   40
First printing, January 2010

One sunny day, Ash, Brock, Dawn, and their Pokémon were in the park. Brock was reading the newspaper.

"Wow! The Scarf Monster is in Solaceon Town," Brock said.

The three friends were heading to Solaceon Town to their friend Angie's Pokémon day care center. Until . . .

"Piplup, pip!" Piplup cried.

Something big was crashing through the trees.

"Come on!" Ash exclaimed.
But the creature had
disappeared.
"I guess our eyes were
playing tricks on us," Ash said.
"Hey, isn't that Angie's
house?" asked Dawn.

The door opened. "It's great to see you guys again!" Angie said. "Come on in!"

Angie's parents were on vacation. She and her Shinx had the place to themselves.

"Have you heard about the Scarf Monster?" Ash asked Angie. "We saw it on the way here!"

"Not again!" cried Angie. "I'll be right back!" She dashed out the door.

Ash, Dawn, and Brock followed Angie through the woods and into a cave.

"The Scarf Monster you saw is a Pokémon I'm raising," Angie told them.

Angie left a big bowl of yummy Poké food out for her Pokémon.

The kids hid behind the bushes to wait for it.

"I think I hear something coming!" Angie said.

A big pink tongue reached for the Poké food.

"It's the Scarf Monster!" Dawn yelled.

"No, it's a Lickilicky!" said Brock.

"Your Lickilicky is the Scarf Monster?" Ash asked Angie.

"Yes," said Angie. "I was looking after a Lickitung while its trainer is away. But while we were training, it evolved!"

"It's never a good thing when a caretaker evolves someone else's Pokémon," said Brock.

"Lickilicky hates being in its Poké Ball," Angie went on. "I've been keeping it in this cave so my mom and dad don't find out what happened."

"But why is Lickilicky wearing that scarf?" asked Dawn.

"Lickilicky is not the smallest Pokémon. So I blow up its collar and pull it around like a balloon," Angie explained.

The kids didn't realize it, but Team Rocket was tracking the Scarf Monster, too. They were in disguise.

"We're reporters for the *Sinnoh Star*," Jessie told Ash and Angie. "Can you help us find the Scarf Monster?"

"Sure!" said Ash. "The Scarf Monster's over there." He and Angie pointed in different directions.

"That's strange even for them," James whispered.

The kids met back in the cave. Angie tied Lickilicky to a rock with a long rope. "Sorry, Lickilicky," she said. "You have to lie low for a while."

The next morning, Lickilicky smelled something sweet in the air — Poké food!

"Mmm. Lickilicky!" it said.

It broke the rope and followed the smell into the woods.

A giant ball of Poké food was waiting for Lickilicky.

Behind the tasty treat was one of Team Rocket's robots!

"The Scarf Monster is falling for our trap!" cried James.

Team Rocket's robot tied up
Lickilicky.
"Liiiiicky!" it cried out.

Ash, Brock, Dawn, and Angie
found Lickilicky just in time.
"Knock it off! That's Angie's
Lickilicky, not yours!" shouted Ash.

"Is that a twerp I hear?"
Jessie said.

"This robot can handle
those guys, have no fear,"
Meowth replied.

"That's what you think!"
Ash cried.

Pikachu slammed them
with Iron Tail. *Pow!*

Shinx snuck in with Quick
Attack. *Wham!*

Piplup poked them with
Peck. *Pop!*

But the battle had just begun.
"Angie, take care of Lickilicky
while we distract Team Rocket!"
Brock suggested.

"Great idea!" Angie said. She and Ash untied Lickilicky.

"Okay, let's get out of here!" Brock yelped.

"Not so fast!" Meowth
sneered.
Team Rocket's robot
was ready to hurl a giant
rock at them.

"Quick, Lickilicky, use Roll Out!" Angie screamed.
    Bam! Lickilicky knocked over Team Rocket's robot.

"Awesome!" Angie cried.
"Follow it up with Wrap!"
Thwap! Lickilicky tied Team
Rocket up with its tongue.

"Pikachu, you know what to do!" called Ash.

"Pikaaaachuuuuu!"
Pikachu zapped Team Rocket with Thunderbolt.

"We're blasting off again!"
Team Rocket sighed as they
flew through the air.
　　"Great work, buddy! Now
let's go home," Angie said.

"You've done a great job raising Lickilicky, Angie!" Ash said.

"Thanks," said Angie. "But how am I going to explain Lickilicky to my mom and dad?"

"Let's tell them together," Ash said.

"I'm so sorry!" Angie told
her parents.

"We understand," Angie's
mom said. "Lickilicky's trainer
will be here soon. You can tell
him what happened."

Just then, they heard voices outside the window.

"Wowee, look at my beautiful Lickilicky!" the trainer exclaimed.

"The trainer isn't upset that Lickitung evolved. He's thrilled!" said Dawn.

Angie was grateful to her pals
for all their help. "Thanks, guys!"
    "That's what friends are for!"
said Ash.